¡Podemos hacerlo! / We Can Do It!

LISTOS PARA LA ESCUELA / GETTING READY FOR SCHOOL

By Lois Fortuna
Traducido por Nathalie Beullens-Maoui

Please visit our website, www.garethstevens.com. For a free color catalog of all our high-quality books, call toll free 1-800-542-2595 or fax 1-877-542-2596.

Cataloging-in-Publication Data

Fortuna, Lois.
Getting ready for school = Listos para la escuela / Lois Fortuna.
pages cm. — (We can do it! = ¡Podemos hacerlo!)
Parallel title: ¡Podemos hacerlo!.
In English and Spanish.
Includes index.
ISBN 978-1-4824-4360-8 (library binding)
1. School children—Juvenile literature. 2. Morning—Juvenile literature. I. Title.
LB1556.F67 2016
372—dc23

First Edition

Published in 2016 by
Gareth Stevens Publishing
111 East 14th Street, Suite 349
New York, NY 10003

Editor: Ryan Nagelhout
Designer: Laura A. Bowen

Photo credits: Cover, pp. 1, 9, 11, 13, 15, 19, 21 Monkey Business Images/Shutterstock.com; p. 5 littleny/Shutterstock.com; p. 7 sacura/Shutterstock.com; p. 17 maradonna 8888/Shutterstock.com; p. 23 Dan Kosmayer/Shutterstock.com.

Printed in the United States of America

CPSIA compliance information: Batch #CW16GS: For further information contact Gareth Stevens, New York, New York at 1-800-542-2595.

Contenido

Vamos a la escuela 4
Vestirse 8
El uniforme de Nathan 14
¡Listos para partir! 20
Palabras que debes aprender 24
Índice 24

Contents

Time for School 4
Getting Dressed 8
Nathan's Uniform. 14
Ready to Go! 20
Words to Know 24
Index. 24

¡Hoy tengo escuela!
Tengo que prepararme.

I have school today!
I need to get ready.

Primero tomo el desayuno.

First I eat breakfast.

Mamá me ayuda
a vestirme.

My mom helps me
get dressed.

Me pongo un vestido azul.

I wear a blue dress.

Mamá me cepilla
el pelo.

My mom brushes
my hair.

Mi hermano Nathan
también se prepara.

My brother Nathan
gets ready, too.

Se pone camisa
y corbata.
Es su uniforme.

He wears a dress shirt
and tie.
This is called a uniform.

Mi mamá le arregla
la corbata negra.

My mom fixes his
black tie.

Estamos listos para ir
a la escuela.

We are ready to go
to school.

¡Ahora espero
el autobús!

Now I have to
wait for the bus!

SCHOOL BUS

Palabras que debes aprender/ Words to Know

(el) vestido/ dress

(la) corbata/ tie

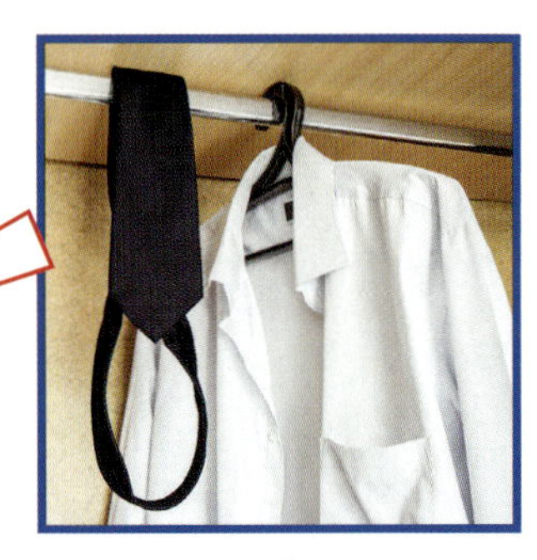

(el) uniforme/ uniform

Índice/Index

autobús/bus 22

corbata/tie 16, 18

escuela/school 4, 20

uniforme/uniform 16